STAR WARS.

ADVENTURES

Podrace to Freedom
GAME BOOK

STAR WARS.

ADVENTURES
GAME BOOK

Podrace to Freedom

A.L. Singer

SCHOLASTIC INC.

New York • Toronto • London • Auckland • Sydney
Mexico City • New Delhi • Hong Kong • Buenos Aires

ISBN 0-439-45897-8

12 11 10 9 8 7 6 5 4 3 2   4 5 6 7 8/0

Printed in the U.S.A.

First Scholastic printing, October 2000

Podrace to Freedom

YOUR ADVENTURE
BEGINS

For the full story behind your adventure, read up to page 12 in your *Star Wars* Adventures Novel, *Podrace to Freedom*. Or begin here.

The Adventure Guide includes the rules for your Star Wars Adventures. You must follow these rules at all times.

You are a kid on the planet Tatooine. Four customers—a man, a girl, an amphibian, and an R2 droid—enter the junk shop where you work. They don't seem like much at first. You've seen all types of customers come into your owner's shop— gangsters and farmers, fugitives and thieves, pilots and Podracers. But the routine is always the same: Your boss will sell. You will fetch. The customers will leave with less than what they paid for.

It is the way of Mos Espa.

And it's all you know.

You were born nine years ago to a slave woman—which means you've been owned since birth. You have never known a father. Your world is a dusty frontier. Your dream is to enter and win the Boonta Eve Podrace. It is the only way a lowly slave can attain some measure of glory. In your fantasies, you've visited the vast reaches of the galaxy, but in reality you know you'll be working here until you die.

Unless something *miraculous* happens.

Right now in the junkyard, your boss is haggling with the man over a T-14 hyperdrive generator, while the girl and the amphibian wait in the shop. You get to know them. The amphibian's annoying. She's amazing. Her name is Padmé, and although she looks way too Inner Core to be in this rough place, she's friendly. Most of all, she treats you like a real person, not a slave.

But your conversation is cut short. The man storms away, angry at your boss—and Padmé must go.

You have a funny feeling about her—about all of them, really. Something tells you their visit was about more than just a T-14 hyperdrive generator.

Your mission is threefold: You must find these people again, find out why they're here, and enter and win the Boonta Eve Podrace. Because you have another feeling—

that all these things will affect what your future holds.

Choose your character. Each character has unique talents that are listed on his or her character card. You can take no more than three devices and you can only use Power three times on this adventure.

You start this adventure with your Adventure Point (AP) total from your previous adventure, or 1000 AP if this is your first adventure.

May the Force be with you.

YOUR ADVENTURE:

PODRACE TO FREEDOM

Your boss has let you out early. As you race home through the sandy, wind-blown streets of Mos Espa, a vendor's sudden shout makes you stop. Across the crowded plaza, the amphibian you met earlier stands frozen in front of a stall, caught in the act of stealing food—its long, ropelike tongue stuck to a fresh-killed gorg that won't come loose from the rack where it hangs.

"Hey, that will be seven wupiupi!" the food vendor shouts.

Thwwwwack!

The amphibian jumps back. The gorg snaps away, breaking its line. It ricochets across the plaza, hurtles into the outdoor café, and plops into a soup bowl with a messy splash.

You cringe when you see to whom the bowl belongs—Sebulba.

Sebulba is evil. He dominates the Outer Rim Podraces, and his enemies have a funny way of crashing whenever they get too close. He looks and smells like dried skin draped over salvaged carcass bones, and his voice sounds like glass scraping metal.

"Ni chuba na?" *Is this yours?*

As Sebulba holds up the gorg, a crowd from around the plaza gathers to watch.

The rubbery amphibian, for the first time since you have met him, is speechless.

With a flick of his arm, Sebulba tosses the hapless creature aside. He falls to the ground in a cloud of dust.

You must step in and save the strange creature. Choose either to fight Sebulba or persuade Sebulba, with or without using Power.

To fight Sebulba: Roll the 20-dice. Your roll# + your strength# + your stealth# is your adventure#.

If your adventure# is equal to or more than 15, add the difference + 10 to your AP total. Mustering up all your courage, you step in front of Sebulba and give him a sharp push. He backs away, grumbling in Huttese: "Next time we race, wermo, it will be the end of you!" His breath is worse than his bite, so you take the fallen amphibian by the arm and calmly proceed.

If your adventure# is less than 15, subtract the difference from your AP total. You step in front of Sebulba, and his putrid breath nearly knocks you out. "Step aside, wermo!" he shouts as he brushes you away with a flick of his leathery arm. You must now proceed to persuade him with or without using Power (below).

To persuade Sebulba (using Power):
Choose your Persuasion Power. Roll the 20-dice. If calm is one of your talents, your roll# + your strength# + your Power# + your Power's mid-resist# + 1 is your adventure#. If calm is not one of your talents, your roll# + your strength# + your Power# + your Power's mid-resist# is your adventure#.

If your adventure# is equal to or more than 14, add the difference + 8 to your AP total. You help the alien up by its arm. Then, turning to Sebulba, you say defiantly, "We're leaving—plan to do something about it?" Sebulba, seeing an opportunity to advertise his upcoming races, backs down and threatens to beat you in the next Podrace. Unafraid, you turn away. You may proceed.

If your adventure# is less than 14, subtract the difference from your AP total. You fix

Sebulba with a steady, confident gaze. Then, calmly, you pick up the alien by its arm. But Sebulba rears back and gives you a good, swift kick. "He's mine, wermo!" he growls, grabbing the amphibian. Now you must try to persuade Sebulba without using Power (below).

*NOTE: This counts as one of three Power uses you are allowed on this adventure.

To persuade Sebulba (without Power): Roll the 20-dice. If charm is one of your talents, your roll# + your charm# + 2 is your adventure#. If charm is not one of your talents, your roll# + your charm# + 1 is your adventure#.

If your adventure# is equal to or more than 13, add the difference + 10 to your AP total. Calmly, you lie and warn Sebulba that the amphibian is well connected to the Hutts— and that you'd hate to see Sebulba diced before you race again. Sebulba shrinks away, muttering, "Next time we race, wermo, it will be the end of you!" His breath is worse than his bite, so you take the fallen creature by the arm and proceed.

If your adventure# is less than 13, subtract the difference from your AP total. "If you beat me now, you'll have to pay my boss for me," you say, fixing Sebulba with a steady gaze, "and you'll never get the chance to prove you can beat me in the Podrace." Snickering, Sebulba just swats you aside. Roll the 10-dice. Your new roll# + your charm# + 1 is your new adventure#.

If your new adventure# is equal to or more than 7, add the difference to your AP total. You lie and warn Sebulba that the amphibian is well connected to the Hutts—and that you'd hate to see Sebulba diced before you race again. Sebulba shrinks away, muttering, "Next time we race, wermo, it will be the end of you!" His breath is worse than his bite, so you take the alien by its arm and proceed.

If your new adventure# is less than 7, subtract 20 from your AP total. Sebulba throws the battered, soup-slimed gorg at you. You jump away, but it hits you on the head with a loud squish. As the crowd bursts out laughing, Sebulba gloats, "I'll humiliate you even worse at the next Podrace, wermo!" Wiping soup out of your hair, you take the amphibian by its arm and slink away. Subtract 1 from your charm# for the remainder of this adventure and proceed.

As you leave, you see the amphibian's friends—Padmé, the man, and the R2 droid—working their way through the crowd.

"Hi!" you call out. "Your buddy here was about to be turned into orange goo. He picked a fight with a Dug—an especially dangerous Dug called Sebulba."

"Mesa haten crunchen," the alien says. "Dat's da last thing mesa wanten."

The man glances at him sternly. "Nevertheless, the boy is right. You're heading into trouble. Thank you, my young friend."

He's a man of few words, forceful and commanding. A thank you from him really feels like something.

As you head out of the plaza with the small group, the amphibian murmurs, "Mesa do-en nutten..."

At the edge of the plaza you spot a friend—Jira, the old fruit seller. Unlike so many of the other vendors, the years of poverty and hard work haven't made her hard and bitter.

"I'll take four pallies today." You glance at your new friends. "You'll like these."

You pay Jira and give the man a pallie. He looks distracted as he opens his cloak to put it in a belt compartment.

Something peeks out from his cloak. Something silver and shiny that you recognize immediately.

A laser sword.

Your breath catches in your throat.

He is no farmer. Farmers don't carry devices like that.

Only one group of people does. The greatest heroes in the galaxy. The Jedi Knights, whose legends were only whispers of glory by the time they reached Tatooine.

But you know that kind of person never comes here. Never in a billion years. Tatooine is an outpost for the thieving, the desperate—and people with stolen goods to sell.

At the edge of the plaza, you can see the stiffening wind make sand clouds over the desert. Behind you an awning gives a loud *snap* as the merchants try to quickly close shop.

"Do you have shelter?" you ask the strangers.

"We'll head back to our ship," the farmer (the Jedi!) replies.

"Is it far?"

"On the outskirts."

"You'll never reach the outskirts in time. Sandstorms are very, very dangerous. Come with me—*hurry*!"

The sand flies into your eyes and mouth as you leave the plaza. The storm is moving closer by the second. It'll be hard enough just to get home.

It's up to you to get your new friends through the sandstorm without becoming buried.

To get everyone home through the sandstorm: Roll the 20-dice. Your roll# + your navigation# + your stealth# is your adventure#.

If your adventure# is equal to or more than 14, add the difference + 12 to your AP total. You break into a run, making sure the others follow. You take a winding path, keeping to streets that are sheltered from the wind. Because visibility is low, you shout directions as you go. Soon you reach the slave quarters. All of your new friends are accounted for. You may proceed.

If your adventure# is less than 14, subtract the difference from your AP total. There is sand is in your eyes. You try to take a path home through sheltered streets, but you lose your way—and you run right into a wandering Tatooine rogue. The sandstorm has brought out his fighting spirit, and he attacks you. Choose to either fight the rogue or run from the rogue.

To fight the rogue: Roll the 20-dice. If defense is one of your talents, your roll# + your strength# + 2 is your adventure#. If defense is not one of your talents, your roll# + your strength# is your adventure#.

If your adventure# is equal to or more than 14, add the difference + 9 to your AP total. Your assailant's mask may protect his face, but he still can't see well in the blowing sand. You drop to the ground and tackle him by the ankles. He falls over, shrieking with surprise. Then he scrambles to his feet and cries "Peedunkel!"—a Huttese insult—as he runs away. He knows not to mess with the likes of you. You may proceed.

If your adventure# is less than 14, subtract the difference from your AP total. You take your hands from your face and push the rogue. But the sand batters your eyes—and you tumble to the ground. To try getting away, roll the 10-dice.

> *If you roll 1, 2, 3, or 4,* you scramble to your feet. The rogue's mask may protect his face, but he still can't see well in the blowing sand. You drop to the ground and tackle him by the ankles. He falls over, shrieking with surprise. Then he scrambles to his feet and cries "Peedunkel!"—a Huttese insult—as he runs away. He knows not to mess with the likes of you. You may proceed.

> *If you roll 5, 6, 7, or 8,* the rogue looms above you, swinging his fists—but he can't see you well in the blowing sand. You must run (below).

> *If you roll 9 or 0,* the rogue begins to pound you with his fists and feet. You scramble away, but he follows you. Finally, your new friend, the farmer, steps in and chases the rogue away. Your

companions help you to your feet, but you have been seriously injured. Subtract 1 from your strength# for the remainder of this adventure and try not to get injured again. You may proceed.

To run from the rogue: Roll the 20-dice. If evasion is one of your talents, your roll# + your stealth# + 3 is your adventure#. If evasion is not one of your talents, your roll# + your stealth# + 1 is your adventure#.

If your adventure# is equal to or more than 12, add the difference + 10 to your AP total. If you rise to his bait, you may not make it home before the sand buries you. With a burst of speed, you and your companions leave the rogue in a cloud of sand and his own stupidity. You may proceed.

If your adventure# is less than 12, subtract the difference from your AP total. You try to duck away, but you're not quite fast enough. The rogue steps in front of you, fists raised. You have no choice but to go back "To fight the rogue" (above).

You wind your way through the crowded slave quarter to your sandstone home. It's small, but there's enough room for the strangers to wait out the storm in comfort.

"Mom!" you call out. "I'm home!"

The amphibian gazes around approvingly. "Disen cozy!"

Your mother enters from your room. She wears a rough-spun gray tunic and keeps her hair in the simple, pulled-back style typical of a Mos Espa slave.

To you, she is the most beautiful woman in the world.

"Oh, my!" she exclaims, staring at the strange group. "What's this?"

"These are my friends, Mom. This is Padmé, and...gee, I don't know the rest of your names."

"I'm Qui-Gon Jinn," says the man, who then gestures to the amphibian. "And this is Jar Jar Binks."

The little droid beeps.

"And our droid, Artoo-Detoo," Padmé says.

"*I'm* building a droid," you blurt out. "Want to see?"

Your mom looks at you curiously. "Why are they here?"

"A sandstorm, Mom," you explain. "Listen."

In the silence, the room echoes with the howl of the approaching wind.

"Your child was kind enough to offer us shelter," Qui-Gon says.

You take Padmé's arm. "Come on, let me show you Threepio!"

You speed into your room, pulling Padmé with you.

On a workbench by the wall lies C-3PO, your pride and joy—a standard cybot protocol droid. New, the droids are incredibly expensive. But because you know where to find parts, you've been building your own for free.

"Isn't he great?" you say. "I'm not finished yet."

"He's wonderful!" Padmé exclaims.

"You really like him? He's a protocol droid—to help Mom. Watch."

You push the droid's activation switch, but nothing happens. The ignition has been acting up lately, and you've had this problem many times. Choose to either continue hitting the switch, or to fix C-3PO.

To continue hitting the switch: Roll the 10-dice. Your roll# + your skill# + 1 is your adventure#.

If your adventure# is equal to or more than 8, add the difference + 9 to your AP total. You hit the switch again, and C-3PO beeps to life. But you see a spark from the movement sensor wiring, and you make a mental note to fix it later. You may proceed.

If your adventure# is less than 8, subtract the difference from your AP total. You flick the switch rapidly about twenty times. C-3PO beeps and fizzes and cries, "Oh, dear!" before falling into a cloud of smoke. Proceed to fix C-3PO (below).

To fix C-3PO: Roll the 20-dice. If repair is one of your talents, your roll# + your skill# + your knowledge# + 2 is your adventure#. If repair is not one of your talents, your roll# + your skill# + your knowledge# is your adventure#.

If your adventure# is equal to or more than 15, add the difference + 9 to your AP total. Examining C-3PO's chest, you see a loose movement sensor wire. You remove the wire, put it in your pocket, then carefully choose the same gauge wire to replace it. C-3PO starts like new. You may proceed.

If your adventure# is less than 15, subtract the difference from your AP total. Examining C-3PO's chest, you see a loose movement sensor wire. You remove the wire, put it in your pocket, then grab the first new wire you see. But when you flick his switch, nothing happens. Must be the wrong gauge wire. Go back "To fix C-P3O," and continue trying until you get him going (above).

With a beep and a whir and a blinking of his only working photoreceptor eye, C-3PO sits up.

The other eye is still lying on the work-table. You pull it out of the mess and plug it into its mount frame on C-3PO's face.

"How do you do?" the droid greets you in a soft, cultivated voice. "I am See-Threepio, Human-Cyborg relations. How might I serve you?"

"He's perfect," Padmé says admiringly.

"When the storm is over, you can see my racer!" you blurt out. "I'm building a Podracer!"

You like Padmé's smile—sincere, admiring, intelligent, not at all like the "isn't-he-a-smart-little-kid" kind of smile you're so used to seeing.

But before you can continue, R2-D2 begins whistling and beeping at the protocol droid.

"I beg your pardon," C-3PO says, "what do you mean, I'm *naked*?"

R2-D2's beeps and whistles grow more animated.

C-3PO recoils. "My *parts* are showing? My goodness, how embarrassing!"

You and Padmé move into the main room to avoid laughing out loud and upsetting C-3PO even more.

Your good mood stops when you hear the violent shriek of the wind outside—and when you see Qui-Gon by himself in a corner.

He is speaking into a comlink in hushed tones. But a fragment of his conversation reaches your ears: "What if the message is true, and the people are dying?"

You can't get the remark out of your mind as you help prepare dinner.

Dinner is a bit strained. Not only because of the weather, but because of Jar Jar's eating habits.

SSSSHKKKLLLLLLIIISSHHHHP!

The sound of the amphibian's soup-slurping is like some backed-up plumbing device. Your mother winces but continues eating. The others glare at him. He sinks back in his seat.

You barely notice. Your mind is on other things.

The people are dying, you think. *What does it mean? What people? Why is Qui-Gon worried about matters like that?*

Now, as you eat dinner to the raging music of the winds, Qui-Gon is asking about the life of a Mos Espan slave.

"...All slaves have transmitters placed inside their bodies somewhere," your mother explains.

You snap back into the conversation. "I've been working on a scanner to try to locate the transmitters, but no luck."

Your mother sighs. "Any attempt to escape..."

"And they blow you up," you add. "*Boom!*"

Jar Jar gasps. "How wude!"

"I can't believe there is still slavery in the galaxy," Padmé says with bewilderment. "The Republic's antislavery laws—"

"The Republic doesn't exist out here," your mother says. "We must survive on our own."

You hate conversations like this. Visitors, especially those from the Inner Core, never understand the ways of Tatooine.

You don't need anyone's sympathy or pitying looks. *Slave* isn't the word that defines you. And Tatooine isn't where your life will begin and end.

It's time to change the dinner conversation. "Have you ever seen a Podrace?" you ask Padmé.

She shakes her head no.

Sssssssthhhhwirlp!

Jar Jar's tongue shoots out like a whip, snaring some food on the other side of the table. Your mother tries to hold back her dismay.

Qui-Gon gives him a scolding look, but politely continues, "They have Podracing on Malastare. Very fast. *Very* dangerous."

You sit up proudly. "I'm the only human who can do it."

Your mother looks sharply at you.

Qui-Gon looks bemused. "You must have Jedi reflexes if you race Pods."

Ssstthhhh—

Just as Jar Jar unfurls his lightning-quick tongue, Qui-Gon reaches out with astonishing speed and grabs it between his fingers.

Jar Jar gags.

"Don't do that again," Qui-Gon says firmly.

"Mmmphwwrppl," Jar Jar mumbles, nodding.

Qui-Gon releases his fingers and the tongue snaps back.

Amazing. No one—not a human alive—can have reflexes like *that*.

Well, almost no one.

"I—I am wondering something..." you begin.

"What?" Qui-Gon asks.

"Well, ahhh..." You take a deep breath. "You're a Jedi Knight, aren't you?"

"What makes you think that?"

"I saw your laser sword. Only Jedi carry that kind of weapon."

Qui-Gon leans back and smiles nonchalantly. "Perhaps I killed a Jedi and took it from him."

"I don't think so. No one can kill a Jedi!"

"I wish that were so...."

"I had a dream I was a Jedi—I came back here and freed all the slaves." You look Qui-Gon straight in the eye. "Have you come to free us?"

"No," Qui-Gon replies. "I'm afraid not."

"I think you have. Why else would you be here?"

Qui-Gon thinks for a long moment. His eyes seem to burrow through you, making you feel warm and cold at the same time. Finally, he leans forward across the table. "I can see there's no fooling you. You mustn't let anyone know about us. We're on our way to Coruscant, the central system in the Republic, on a very important mission. And it must be kept secret."

"Coruscant?" The name is magical to you—the seat of the Galactic Republic, the grandest of planets. "Wow—how did you end up out here in the Outer Rim?"

"Our ship is damaged," Padmé explains, "and we're stranded here until we can repair it."

"I can help!" you say eagerly. "I can fix anything!"

"I believe you can," Qui-Gon assures you, "but our first job is to acquire the parts we need."

"Wit no-nutten moola to trade," Jar Jar adds glumly.

"These junk dealers must have a weakness of some kind," Padmé interjects.

Your mother nods. "Gambling. Everything here revolves around betting on those awful races."

"Podracing..." Qui-Gon sits back, thinking. "Greed can be a powerful ally."

"I've built a racer!" you exclaim. "It's the fastest ever. There's a big race tomorrow, on Boonta Eve. You can enter my Pod. It's all but finished!"

"Now, settle down," your mother says. "The boss won't let you —"

"He doesn't know I've built it!" You look pleadingly at Qui-Gon. "You can make him think it's yours, and you can get him to let me pilot it for you."

Your mother's face darkens. "I don't want you to race. It's awful. I die every time you do it."

You have to race! Choose to either convince your mother to let you race with or without using Power.

To convince your mother to let you race (using Power)*: Choose your Persuasion Power. Roll the 20-dice. Your roll# + your charm# + your Power# + your Power's mid-resist# + 1 is your adventure#.

If your adventure# is equal to or more than 14, add the difference + 7 to your AP total. You tell your mom that you need to help your friends—your prize money will pay for the parts they need. She's still not convinced, so you remind her of what she's always told you: "The biggest problem in the universe is that no one helps each other." Her eyes start to tear. You know she will agree. You may proceed.

If your adventure# is less than 14, subtract the difference from your AP total. You tell your mom that your prize money will pay for the parts your friends need. You remind her of what she's always told you: "The biggest problem in the universe is that no one helps each other." But just as she's about to cry, Jar Jar lets out a great Gungan belch, and the moment is ruined. To try and convince her again, roll the 10-dice. Your new roll# + your charm# + your Power# + your Power's low-resist# + 1 is your new adventure#.

If your new adventure# is equal to or more than 12, add the difference to your AP total. You continue to talk to her about how much the Jedi need your help, and how important it is to help people in need. Eventually, she's won over. You may proceed.

If your new adventure# is less than 12, subtract the difference from your AP total. You plead with your mother, but her feeling for your safety is stronger than your Power, and she still says no. Finally, Qui-Gon speaks up: "Your mother's right. Is there anyone friendly to the Republic who might be able to help us?" Proceed to try and convince your mother to let you race (without using Power), (below).

*NOTE: This counts as one of three Power uses you are allowed on this adventure.

To convince your mother to let you race (without using Power): Roll the 20-dice. If charm is one of your talents, your roll# + your charm# + 1 is your adventure#. If charm is not one of your talents, your roll# + your charm# is your adventure#.

If your adventure# is equal to or more than 13, add the difference + 10 to your AP total. You tell your mom that you need to help your friends—your prize money will pay for the parts they need. She's still not convinced, so you remind her of what she's always told you: "The biggest problem in the universe is that no one helps each other." Her eyes start to tear. You know she will agree. You may proceed.

If your adventure# is less than 13, subtract 10 from your AP total. You get up from the table, fold your arms across your chest, and announce that you won't eat another morsel of food ever in your whole life if she doesn't say yes. She tells you to go to your room. Roll the 10-dice.

> *If you roll 1, 2, 3, or 4*, go to your room and stew for a few minutes. You feel awful. You've got to learn to control your temper. Just as you are about to go back out and apologize, your mother comes in and asks you to return to the table. She has something to say to you and Qui-Gon. You may proceed.

> *If you roll 5 or 6*, get yourself together, go back out to the kitchen, apologize—

and proceed to convince your mother to let you race (using Power), above.

If you roll 7, 8, 9, or 0, go back to "Roll the 10-dice" and keep trying to convince your mother until you're successful.

Tears rim your mother's eyes as she says to Qui-Gon, "There is no other way. I may not like it, but my child can help you." Her voice drops almost to a whisper. "My child was...*meant* to help you."

Your jaw drops. "Is that a yes? *That is a YES!*"

You have achieved your goal of entering the Boonta Eve Podrace. Add 80 to your AP total.

The next day, you tell your boss that you're entering the race. He doesn't like the idea. Not because of your safety. Or even because the training will take away from your work time in the shop. It's a question, as always, of money.

You and he are practically shouting at one another as Qui-Gon and Padmé walk into the junk shop.

Your boss flies over to the visitors. "The child tells me you want to sponsor him in a race," he says. "You can't afford *parts*. How can you do this? Not on Republic credits, I think."

"My ship," Qui-Gon replies, "will be the entry fee."

From a pocket, he pulls out a disc-shaped holoprojector and holds it before your boss. An image of the Queen's Royal Starship instantly appears, hovering ghostlike over the disk.

Your boss studies it carefully, nodding his head. "Not bad...not bad...a Nubian..."

"It's in good order," Qui-Gon says, "except for the parts we need."

"But what will the child ride?" your boss asks. "He smashed up my Pod in the last race. It will take some long time to fix it."

You swallow hard. You were hoping your boss wouldn't mention that. "It wasn't my fault, really. Sebulba flashed me with his vent ports. I actually *saved* the Pod...mostly."

"That you did," your boss says with a

chuckle. "The child is good, no doubts there."

"I have acquired a Pod in a game of chance," Qui-Gon reports. "The fastest ever built."

Your boss lets out a sudden belly laugh. "I hope you didn't kill anyone I know for it. So, *you* supply the Pod and the entry fee, and *I* supply the child. We split the winnings—fifty-fifty, I think."

"Fifty-fifty?" Qui-Gon retorts. "If it's going to be fifty-fifty, I suggest you front the cash for the entry. If we win, you keep all the winnings, minus the cost of the parts I need. If we lose, you keep my ship."

Your boss falls silent, thinking. Your heart races. Your boss is a gambler—but he is also unpredictable. He only bets on his terms. And when he decides no, he cannot be convinced otherwise.

"Either way, you win," Qui-Gon prods.

"Deal!" your boss finally says. With a big smile, he turns to you. "Yo bana pee ho-tah, meendee ya!" *Your friend is a foolish one, methinks.*

After work you run home, confident that your Podracer needs only a little work to be shipshape. Your best friends on Tatooine are coming over this afternoon. For months, they've been laughing at your broken-down Podracer. You want to be ready to rev the engines and watch their jaws drop!

The moment you arrive, you and the droids get to work. Padmé and Jar Jar watch from a distance. Immediately, you discover two leaky energy binder couplings. They're the wrong size. You must run and find new parts or try to fix the couplings yourself. Choose to either search for new parts or fix the couplings yourself.

To search for new parts: Roll the 20-dice. Your roll# + your skill# + your knowledge# + 1 is your adventure#.

If your adventure# is equal to or more than 15, add the difference + 8 to your AP total. You grab the couplings along with a rare Dorian spaceship part from your junk collection and race back to the plaza, where you find a band of Jawas. Because you offer them the rare part, they gladly exchange the couplings for the correct size—and they throw in spare connecting wires. After running home and quickly installing them, you may proceed.

If your adventure# is less than 15, subtract the difference from your AP total. You grab the couplings and race back to the Jawa camp. You scold them for selling you the wrong size and demand an exchange. Frostily they shake their heads, saying they have a no-return policy on used goods. You've lost time! You must proceed to run home and try to fix the couplings yourself (below).

To fix the couplings yourself: Roll the 20-dice. If repair is one of your talents, your roll# + your skill# + your knowledge# + 2 is your adventure#. If repair is not one of your talents, your roll# + your skill# + your knowledge# is your adventure#.

If your adventure# is equal to or more than 15, add the difference + 11 to your AP total. You find a welding tool, don a mask, and try to weld the couplings to the binders. R2-D2 beeps and splutters merrily, complimenting you on your skills. The moment you finish, you hear your friends running toward you. You may proceed.

If your adventure# is less than 15, subtract the difference from your AP total. You find a welding tool, don a mask, and try to weld the couplings to the binders. Your welding skills are rusty. R2-D2 seems to want to help, but you insist on doing it yourself—and manage to melt the connecting wires. To continue working, roll the 10-dice.

> *If you roll 1, 2, 3, or 4*, you must run to search for new parts (above).

> *If you roll 5, 6, 7, or 8*, you replace the connecting wires and try fixing the couplings again, with R2-D2's help. Together, you weld the couplings until they're perfect. You may proceed.

> *If you roll 9 or 0*, frustrated, you let R2-D2 do the work—and he fixes the couplings like new. Subtract 1 from your skill# for the rest of this adventure. You may proceed.

Your best friend bounds into the courtyard. Behind him are two other human friends, Seek and Amee, and a green-skinned, snouted Rodian named Wald.

You quickly introduce them to Padmé, Jar Jar, C-3PO, and R2-D2.

Your best friend leans down to inspect R2-D2. "Wow, a real Astro droid. How'd you get so lucky?"

"That isn't the half of it," you reply eagerly. "I'm entered in the Boonta Eve Podrace tomorrow!"

"What—with *this*?" your best friend says, gesturing dismissively toward the Podracer.

"Jesko na joka," Wald adds. *You are such a joke.*

"You've been working on that thing for years," Amee says. "It's never going to run."

Seek turns to go. "Come on, let's play ball. Keep it up, you're going to be bug squash!"

Amee and Wald follow, laughing.

You don't mind. You'll show them....

The Podracer is an old-style model, with an arrowhead-shaped cockpit connected by long cables to two afterthrusters. In its day, this model was the most flexible and speedy of them all. Retrofitted with the modern equipment you've collected, it will be a contender again.

As you return to your work, you notice Jar Jar tinkering near the energy binders. "Hey, Jar Jar! Stay away from those!"

Jar Jar looks up with a start. "Who, mesa?"

"If your hand gets caught in that beam, it will go numb for hours."

Dzzzzt!

A bolt of electricity zaps Jar Jar in the mouth. "Ouch! Dssssuyviigouuso..." he mumbles, trying to massage some feeling back into his lips as he slinks away.

The binder energy gauge has dipped sharply. Jar Jar must have triggered the emergency shutoff. You try to override it, but the turbine's energy just peters out. The override mechanism on this model, which allows the turbines to run even if something is caught between them, is delicate and difficult to fix. And it's better to disable it, despite the potential danger. You don't imagine anyone will be stupid enough to stand between the engines again. Not even

Jar Jar. Choose to either fix the override or disable the override.

To fix the override: Roll the 20-dice. If repair is one of your talents, your roll# + your skill# + your knowledge# + 2 is your adventure#. If repair is not one of your talents, your roll# + your skill# + your knowledge# is your adventure#.

If your adventure# is equal to or more than 15, add the difference + 9 to your AP total. You connect new, sturdier wires, and R2-D2 threads them through all of the places that your hands can't reach. The override is now working better than it ever has. You may proceed.

If your adventure# is less than 15, subtract 11 from your AP total. You refuse to let R2-D2 help you rewire the mechanism, and you cause a short-circuit. Now you have to completely disable the override (below).

To disable the override: Roll the 20-dice. Your roll# + your skill# + your knowledge# is your adventure#.

If your adventure# is equal to or more than 14, add the difference + 10 to your AP total.

The mechanism is delicate, and you must take great care not to disable anything else. You allow R2-D2 to pull out the wiring in all of the places that you can't reach. Soon the override is history, and you may proceed.

If your adventure# is less than 14, subtract the difference from your AP total. You reach in and start yanking out wires. The Podracer sparks, shudders, and goes totally dead. To fix the engine, roll the 10-dice. Your new roll# + your skill# + your knowledge# + 1 is your new adventure#.

If your new adventure# is equal to or more than 9, add the difference to your AP total. With R2-D2's help, you quickly rewire the main engine circuits and carefully rebuild the override mechanism. Your Podracer is now shipshape and safe. You may proceed.

If your new adventure# is less than 9, subtract 50 from your AP total. The electricity kicks back on while you are attempting another override. You are severely shocked. If you have been injured already on this mission, subtract 200 from your AP total, go back to the beginning of this adventure, and start again as another character. If you have not been injured before, subtract 1 from your strength# for the rest of this adventure. R2-D2 fixes the damage and you may proceed.

Your best friend examines the Pod skeptically. "But you don't even know if this thing will run."

"It will," you reply. You have only one thing left to check—the auxiliary power shifter, which tends to jam if you don't let it out at the exact right speed.

"Bibbbbluuuthchaarreesthh…"

You're only vaguely aware of Jar Jar's garbled voice, because you're distracted by the sight of Qui-Gon, who is entering the courtyard holding a new piece of equipment.

"I think it's time we found out if it'll run," Qui-Gon calls out. "Use this power charge."

"Yes, *sir!*" You nearly pounce on the battery, taking it from Qui-Gon's hands and jumping into the cockpit. As you insert it into the dashboard and strap yourself into the pilot's seat, your best friend and Qui-Gon back away.

"RREEUUUUBBBLLLCCHHHEEEBBOOO!"

At the sound of Jar Jar's frantic scream, Padmé runs to the front of the Podracer. Hidden, at first, from your sight, the creature is caught in the engines.

After a self-test of exactly thirty seconds, the engine will automatically ignite. You could try to disable the automatic ignition, but you're not sure you can do it in time. Or you could jump out of the cockpit and try to help Jar Jar, but then both of you may be sucked into the turbines. Choose to either stop the automatic ignition or pull Jar Jar to safety, before he becomes Filet of Gungan.

To stop the automatic ignition: Roll the 20-dice. Your roll# + your skill# + your knowledge# + 2 is your adventure#.

If your adventure# is equal to or more than 15, add the difference + 18 to your AP total. Pulling up the side panels, you locate the auto-ignition and a display panel that reads 14 seconds...then 13...12.... At 9 seconds, you find a reset switch. You help Padmé pull Jar Jar from danger. Then you try to start the engine again—and the countdown begins from scratch. You may proceed.

If your adventure# is less than 15, subtract the difference from your AP total. Pulling up the side panels, you locate the auto-ignition and a display panel that reads 14 seconds... then 13... 12.... Jar Jar is screaming. You begin pulling wires like crazy but nothing happens. To continue trying to save Jar Jar, roll the 10-dice. Your new roll# + your skill# + your knowledge# is your new adventure#.

If your new adventure# is equal to or more than 9, add the difference to your AP total. 9 seconds.... You pull yourself together. Wiping grime off a of set of switches, you notice one that says reset. You flick it and the engine stops. After helping Padmé pull Jar Jar from danger, you rev the engine again. You may proceed.

If your new adventure# is less than 9, subtract the difference from your AP total. You're frantic. The panel says 2 seconds... 1...SELF-TEST COMPLETE...ignite. A moment before the engine roars to life, Padmé pulls Jar Jar away. Subtract 1 from your skill# for the rest of this adventure, and you may proceed.

To pull Jar Jar to safety: Roll the 20-dice. If reflex is one of your talents, your roll# + your strength# + your skill# + 1 is your adventure#. If reflex is not one of your talents, your roll# + your strength# + your skill# is your adventure#.

If your adventure# is equal to or more than 14, add the difference + 15 to your AP total. You race to the Podracer's engines. Jar Jar's fingers are jammed into the turbine rotors. Thinking fast, you grab a can of fossil-oil spray and squirt some into the mechanism. Not only does Jar Jar's hand slide out, but your turbine is nicely lubed. You may proceed.

If your adventure# is less than 14, subtract the difference from your AP total. You yank Jar Jar as hard as you can, but he screams, "Mesa hand comen off!" This isn't working, and you've wasted precious time. You must go back "To stop the automatic ignition," (above).

Five...four...three...two...one...

FFFFOOOOM! The Podracer roars to life.

"It's working!" you shout.

The turbines are tuned and ready. And so are you.

You have successfully fixed your Podracer. Add 95 to your AP total.

It isn't until sunset that you notice the cut on your arm. Actually, Qui-Gon has to point it out to you.

He carefully applies some kind of gel. "Sit still. Let me clean this cut."

As you sit back impatiently, leaning against the stone wall outside your house, you gaze up into the night sky. Now that the storm has cleared, it seems you can see every star in the galaxy. "There are so many," you muse. "Do they all have a system of planets?"

"Most of them," Qui-Gon replies.

"Has anyone been to them all?"

Qui-Gon chuckles. "Not likely."

"I want to be the first one to see all of them—*ouch*!" You jerk back your arm as Qui-Gon wipes away a few drops of blood.

"There, good as new."

"Bedtime!" your mother calls from inside the house.

Qui-Gon transfers a droplet of your blood onto a small chip and takes out his com-link.

"What are you doing?" you ask.

"Checking your blood for infections," Qui-Gon replies.

Strange. No comlink you've ever seen in the shop can do that. "I've never seen—"

"*Come inside*! I'm not going to tell you again!" warns your mother.

"Go on," Qui-Gon says, "you have a big day tomorrow. Good night."

You roll your eyes. It really *is* a pain to be so young sometimes...

Be careful.

You twist in your bed as a dream surrounds you. It's all so real—a war on another planet, dust whipping up under an army of droids, the rumble of transports and tanks, the hum of laser weapons. And at the head of it, a mighty queen. No, not a queen—

Padmé, what are you doing? Who are all these people? You'll be killed—

Your eyes blink open into your bedroom lit by the rising suns of Tatooine—and she is there. Leaning over you in your own room, not commanding troops, not dressed as a queen.

"You were in my dream..." you murmur. "You were leading a huge army."

"I hope not, I hate fighting," Padmé replies, looking at you curiously. "Your mother wants you to clean up. We have to leave soon."

You leap out of bed. This is Boonta Eve—the day of the race. No time to sleep late. "Where's Qui-Gon?"

"He and Jar Jar left already."

Outside, you see the courtyard door open. Your best friend rides in on a reliable-looking eopie, sturdy and long-snouted, and pulls another behind him.

You run outside and help your best friend harness the eopies to the two engines. You have a nagging feeling you've forgotten something, but you can't think of it. After a quick breakfast, your best friend climbs on an eopie with your mom and you and Padmé mount the other. The animals clop forward, R2-D2 pulls the Pod, and C-3PO waddles alongside.

Next stop, the Mos Espa Grand Arena.

Or so you think.

Just around the corner is a gang of nasty-looking Dugs, who surround your little caravan.

Choose to either ignore them and ride by, or confront the Dugs with or without using Power.

To ignore them and ride by: Roll the 20-dice. If calm is one of your talents, your roll# + your stealth# + 1 is your adventure#. If calm is not one of your talents, your roll# + your stealth# is your adventure#.

If your adventure# is equal to or more than 12, add the difference + 10 to your AP total. You sit tall and spur your eopie onward. As the Dugs watch you pass, one of them asks where the "gorg stealer" is. You realize they're after Jar Jar to avenge Sebulba—but you ignore them. Jar Jar is in good hands. "Not here, wermos," you say. You may proceed.

If your adventure# is less than 12, subtract 20 from your AP total. You hesitate, which gives the Dugs courage to move in. They begin taunting you, and one of them pulls you off your eopie. To try and defend yourself, roll the 10-dice.

If you roll 1 or 2, you fall to the ground. Proceed to confront the Dugs using Power (below).

If you roll 3 or 4, one of your friends saves you from the Dugs and manages to chase them away. You may proceed.

If you roll 5, 6, 7, or 8, you fall to the ground. Proceed to confront the Dugs using Power (below).

If you roll 9 or 0, you fall to the ground, landing hard on your hands. An excruciating pain shoots up your arms. You have been seriously injured. If you have been seriously injured already on this adventure, you must subtract 200 from your AP total and start the adventure from the beginning, using another character. If you have not been injured already , subtract 1 from your strength# for the rest of this adventure and try not to get injured again. The Dugs taunt you and strut away toward the arena. You may proceed.

To confront the Dugs (using Power)*: Choose your Confusion or Reflex Power. Roll the 20-dice. Your roll# + your stealth# + your strength# + your Power# + your Power's mid-resist# is your adventure#.

If your adventure# is equal to or more than 16, add the difference + 15 to your AP total. You jump off your eopie. The Dugs surround you, taunting heartlessly. As they pounce, you drop to the ground and roll away. They begin pummeling each other, to the amazement of your friends. You climb back onto your eopie and ride away, leaving your attackers fighting in the dust. You may proceed.

If your adventure# is less than 16, subtract 35 from your AP total. You are about to pounce when your mother stops you. "This is no time for fighting," your mother says, and you can see that she is right. The Dugs disperse, and you may proceed.

*NOTE: This counts as one of three Power uses you are allowed on this adventure.

To confront the Dugs (without using Power): Roll the 20-dice. Your roll# + your stealth# + your strength# + 1 is your adventure#.

If your adventure# is equal to or more than 15, add the difference + 15 to your AP total. You jump off your eopie. A sinister, wrinkly Dug taunts you, while a younger one sneaks behind you. You wait for the precise moment, then spin around and surprise the younger Dug with a sharp kick. Shocked by your fighting ability, the cowardly Dugs retreat.

If your adventure# is less than 15, subtract the difference from your AP total. As you jump, one of the Dugs trips you. Another one leans over you, waving his chin wattles in your face, a traditional Dug gesture of humiliation. To confront the Dugs again, roll the 10-dice. Your new roll# + your stealth# + your strength# is your new adventure#.

If your new adventure# is equal to or more than 8, add the difference + 5 to your AP total. You stand up. A sinister, wrinkly Dug taunts you while the younger one sneaks behind you. You wait for the precise moment, then spin around and surprise the cowardly Dug with a sharp kick. Immediately, the entire group retreats. You may proceed.

If your new adventure# is less than 8, subtract the difference from your AP total. The Dugs begin to kick you, and they taunt you with a screeching chant full of disgusting, guttural noises. The eopies, who have sensative hearing, rear back and bleat loudly. Padmé and your mother run forward to defend you. This scares away the cowardly Dugs. You may proceed.

Entering the hangar, you shiver with excitement. The place is teeming with the droids and crews of all the great Podracers of the Outer Rim. The pilots themselves are milling about, testing equipment. Spidery Gasgano, slippery Ratts Tyerell, stout Teemto Pagalies, skinny Mars Guo, and of course, Sebulba—they're the main contenders. The others, Boles Roor, Ben Quadinaros, Mawhonic, and the rest, are second-raters.

You head toward an empty hangar berth, where your boss and Qui-Gon seem to be in a deep conversation.

"Bonapa keesa pateeso," your boss calls to you cheerfully as you begin flying away. "O wanna meetee chobodd!" *Better stop your friend's betting, or I'll end up owning him, too!*

Strange. You thought Jedi were *above* such activities as betting. "What does he mean by that?" you ask.

"I'll tell you later," Qui-Gon replies.

As you guide the pieces of the Podracer into place, R2-D2 communicates with beeps and whistles to your protocol droid.

"Oh my, space travel sounds rather perilous," C-3PO replies. "I can *assure* you they will never get me onto one of those dreadful starships!"

Your best friend grins at you. "This is so wizard! I'm sure you'll do it this time."

"Do what?" Padmé asks.

"Finish the race, of course!" your best friend replies.

Padmé's eyes widen. "You've never won a race?"

"Well, not exactly..." you say.

"Not even *finished*?"

You shake your head. "But I will this time."

"Of course you will," Qui-Gon agrees.

You have just enough time to check the linkage cables, lube the engines, and test the thrusters before the lineup call blares over the loudspeakers. Once again, you have the nagging feeling that you haven't checked *something*—but at a time like this, you can't get lost in details. With your team, you guide your Podracer slowly out of the hangar and toward Mos Espa Grand Arena.

You can barely keep your feet on the ground.

As you enter, the crowd noise hits you like a sandstorm. The famous arena announcer, a two-headed alien named Fode/Beed, is exciting the crowd in two languages—Basic and Huttese.

"TOOGI! TOOGI! TOONG MEE CHA KULKAH DU BOONTA MAGI, TAH OOS AZALUS OOVAL PODRACES." *We have perfect weather today for the Boonta Eve Classic, the most hazardous of all Podraces.*

"THAT'S ABSOLUTELY RIGHT. AND A BIG TURNOUT HERE, FROM ALL CORNERS OF THE OUTER RIM TERRITORIES. I SEE CONTESTANTS ARE MAKING THEIR WAY OUT TO THE STARTING GRID...."

"POO TULA MOOSTA, WOE GRANEE CHAMPIO SEBULBA DU PIXELITO! SPASTY-LEEYA BOOKIE OOKIE!" *On the front line, the reigning champion, Sebulba from Pixelito! He's by far the favorite today.*

"AND A LATE ENTRY, A LOCAL CHILD."

"WAMPA PEEDUNKEE UNKO." *I hope this one has better luck this time.*

Better luck? This victory will have nothing to do with luck, you vow. *It will be about skill and smarts.*

"I SEE THE FLAGGERS ARE MOVING ONTO THE TRACK...."

As you line up at the start, you see Jabba the Hutt hefting himself into a sky box. In accordance with tradition, you and the other racers step out of your Pods and bow. The crowd cheers wildly.

Jabba is a tremendous tyrant, both in power and size. He reminds you of a pile of Bantha fat wrapped in the casing of a giant slug.

Gesturing grandly, Jabba welcomes the crowd, and Fode/Beed begins to announce

the contestants: "SEBULBA...TUTA PIXELI-
TO!"

The crowd roars. A band plays a fanfare as Sebulba waves.

Your best friend quickly attaches the Pod to the engines and begins to unhook the eopies.

You turn to your mom. She's smiling, but her face is tense. Fearful.

You embrace her tightly. She will have nothing to worry about.

Fode/Beed calls out your name, and you wave to the cheering home crowd.

Jar Jar pats you on the back. "Dis berry scary."

"You carry all our hopes," Padmé says, giving you a soft kiss on the cheek.

"I won't let you down," you reply.

Sebulba totters up beside you. His cheek wattles flap in the wind, and his dry lips turn up hideously in what must be a kind of grin. "Bazda wahota, shag," he says smugly. "Dobiella nok. Yoka to bantha poodoo." *You*

won't walk away from this one, slave scum!
You're bantha poodoo.

He thinks he's pretty clever. Proceed to give him an insult that'll really sting.

To insult Sebulba: Roll the 10-dice. Your roll# + your charm# + your knowledge# is your adventure#.

If your adventure# is equal to or more than 8, add the difference + 10 to your AP total. Without missing a beat, you say, "Cha skrunee da pat, sleemo," which means *Don't count on it, slimeball.* Sebulba is speechless. You may proceed.

If your adventure# is less than 8, subtract the difference from your AP total. Other racers are snickering at Sebulba's insult. You shoot back a clever response—but in your anger, the Huttese words get scrambled into a phrase that means, approximately, *Our sphere contains slime mold.* The racers look at you curiously. To try insulting Sebulba once more, roll the 10-dice again. Your new roll# + your charm# + your knowledge# is your new adventure#.

If your new adventure# is equal to or more than 8, add the difference + 10 to your AP total. Without missing a beat, you say, "Cha skrunee da pat, sleemo," which means, *Don't count on it, slimeball*. Sebulba is speechless. You may proceed.

If your new adventure# is less than 8, subtract the difference from your AP total. In the baffled silence, you take a moment to compose your thoughts. But just as you're about to speak again, several Podracers burst out laughing. You slip into the Pod before Sebulba can see your face turn red. You must control your anger and ignore them. In the end, you will have the last laugh. You may proceed.

"KAA BAZZA KUNDEE HODRUDDA!" Jabba announces. *Let the challenge begin!*

You jump into your seat. The people in the stands are stomping their feet. Crew members shout urgent last-minute instructions, frightened eopies honk, and your best friend lets out a loud whoop of joy.

Qui-Gon has to raise his voice over the din. "Remember, concentrate on the moment. *Feel*, don't think. Trust your instincts." He gives you a fond smile. "May the Force be with you."

You strap on your goggles. You flip the power-coupling activation switch. The engines roar as the energy binders ignite between the two capsules. All around the arena, the sound of revving Podracers fills the air.

Proceed to choose your Podracer now.

Above the track on a bridge, a large light glows red. The flaggers move off the track. Out of the corner of your eye, you see your mother and your new friends rising upward on an elevated viewing platform.

Three laps. Three *long* laps. You'll have to keep your enthusiasm in check, keep enough back for a killer final kick.

"START YOUR ENGINES!" commands Fode/Beed.

GRRRRROMMMMMMM!

As the main engines ignite with a thunderous boom, all eyes focus on Jabba. Following the Hutt tradition, he bites the head off a small creature and spits it out at the gong.

The head bounces.

The gong clangs.

The light turns green.

You jam the accelerator. The engine screams.

And dies.

"THE YOUNG TATOOINIAN HAS STALLED!"

The exhaust from the departed Podracers fills your lungs. You must find out what is wrong with your engines and fix it—immediately. Choose either to fix your engine using the dashboard controls, or by getting out and examining the engines with or without using Power.

To fix your engine using the dashboard controls: Roll the 20-dice. If repair is one of your talents, your roll# + your knowledge# + your skill# + 1 is your adventure#. If repair is not one of your talents, your roll# + your knowledge# + your skill# is your adventure#.

If your adventure# is equal to or more than 14, add the difference + 17 to your AP total. On your vehicle's diagnostic gauge, the right-burner image shows a thrown circuit breaker.

You have a strong hunch about who threw it. You hit the OVERRIDE switch. If you have not disabled the OVERRIDE mechanism previously, you may proceed. If you have disabled the OVERRIDE mechanism previously, you must give back the 17 AP points and get out and examine the engine, without using Power (below).

If your adventure# is less than 14, subtract the difference from your AP total. In frustration, you smash your fists on the dashboard, knocking out your diagnostic gauge. Now you must think of something else—and you've lost precious time. To try fixing your engine again, roll the 10-dice.

> *If you roll 1, 2, 3, or 4,* figuring some safety device or circuit breaker has been inadvertently flipped, you hit the OVERRIDE switch. If you have not disabled the OVERRIDE mechanism previously, you may proceed. If you have disabled the OVERRIDE mechanism previously, subtract 10 points from your AP total and get out and examine the engine, without usnig Power (below).

> *If you roll 5, 6, 7, or 8,* you must try again. Go back to "Roll the 10-dice" (above).

If you roll 9 or 0, a warning light flashes and the engine erupts. The Podracer is dead! If repair is one of your talents, you must subtract 25 from your AP total and fix your engine using Power (below). If repair is not one of your talents, you must subtract 200 from your AP total and start the adventure again from the beginning, using another character.

To fix your engine by getting out and examining your engines (using Power): Choose your Repair Power. Roll the 20-dice. Your roll# + your knowledge# + your skill# + your Power# + your Power's low-resist# is your adventure#.

If your adventure# is equal to or more than 17, add the difference + 18 to your AP total. You hop out, race to the stern, and see that the coupling circuit breaker is shut off. It's probably Sebulba's handiwork. You quickly set everything back to normal, jump back into the Podracer, and start the engine. You may proceed.

If your adventure# is less than 17, subtract 25 from your AP total. You hop out, race to the stern, and see that the coupling circuit breaker has been shut off. Furious, you repair the engine so completely that it starts all by itself, leaving you in the dust. To run after the Podracer, roll the 10-dice.

If you roll 1, 2, 3, 4, or 5, you run after the Podracer. It speeds ahead, out of control, until it becomes caught in the cables of a turbolift. You jump in, put it in reverse, and then charge after the other racers.

If you roll 6, 7, 8, 9, or 0, you run after the Podracer. It speeds ahead, out of control, until it becomes caught in the cables of a turbolift. You stomp your feet and cry out, "No fair!" at the top of your lungs—but when you see the Podracer caught in the turbolift cables, you run after it. Too late. The entire structure crashes down, and a flying buttress clips you on the leg. You have been seriously injured. If you have been seriously injured already on this adventure, you must subtract 200 from your AP total and start the adventure from the beginning, using a different character. If you have not been injured already, subtract 1 from your strength# for the rest of this adventure and try not to get injured again. You see that the Pod is stalled but intact. You jump in and proceed.

*NOTE: This counts as one of three Power uses you are allowed on this adventure.

To fix your engine by getting out and examining your engines (without using Power): Roll the 10-dice. If repair is one of your talents, your roll# + your knowledge# + your skill# + 1 is your adventure#. If repair is not one of your talents, your roll# + your knowledge# + your skill# is your adventure#.

If your adventure# is equal to or more than 9, add the difference + 20 to your AP total. You hop out and race to the stern. The coupling circuit breaker is shut off—and you have a strong hunch who did it. You flick the switch, jump back into the Pod, and start the engine. You may proceed.

If your adventure# is less than 9, subtract 20 from your AP total. You hop out of the Pod and race to the stern. You begin desperately flipping switches left and right. Your Podracer makes a series of gassy noises and starts to smoke. You must use Power to fix it (below). If you have already used Power three times on this adventure, choose to either subtract 200 from your AP total for an additional Power use, or you can subtract 50 from your AP total and restart this adventure from the beginning.

You're in the race. You think of Qui-Gon's words: *Concentrate on the moment. Trust your instincts.*

Instantly, you set the air intakes to MAX and open the throttle all the way.

VVOOOOOOM!

The Podracer takes off.

The others are way ahead. You know that catching them in an old reconstituted Podracer will require a miracle.

But a lot can happen in three laps.

You gun the accelerator, shooting across the desert. The flying sand makes small pits and gullies in your windshield, and your back presses against the seat, flattening the cushion.

In no time you pass the rearmost contestant—Aldar Beedo. The next three—Dud Bolt...Ark Roose...Neva Kee—are in a cluster ahead. Threading your way through them will save time but is incredibly treacherous. Going around them is safer but may cost you the race. Choose to either thread your way through the Podracers or move around the three Podracers.

To thread your way through the Podracers: Roll the 10-dice. If navigation is one of your talents, your roll# + your navigation# + your vehicle's stealth# + 1 is your adventure#. If navigation is not one of your talents, your roll# + your navigation# + your vehicle's stealth# is your adventure#.

If your adventure# is equal to or more than 9, add the difference + 18 to your AP total. You slip between Dud Bolt and Ark Roose. Dud, rattled by this, swerves into Neva, who is knocked out of the race path—and you vamoose past Roose. You may proceed.

If your adventure# is less than 9, subtract the difference from your AP total. You try to poke yourself between Ark Roose and Neva Kee, but you can never fool Neva, who moves right to block you. You swerve again, but now all three of them block your path. They're unified against you. To get away, roll the 20-dice. Your new roll# + your navigation# + your vehicle's stealth# + 1 is your new adventure#.

If your new adventure# is equal to or more than 14, add the difference to your AP total. You use their unity against them. Since they're flying together, you fake right and fly left as they all move at once. You get past them, but they're amateurs. The worst is yet to come. You may proceed.

If your new adventure# is less than 14, subtract 15 from your AP total. You scream and yell, banging on your steering wheel. Your Pod banks sharply upward. Now you *have* to move around the three Podracers (below).

To try to move around the three Podracers: Roll the 20-dice. Your roll# + your navigation# + your vehicle's speed# + your vehicle's stealth# is your adventure#.

If your adventure# is equal to or more than 16, add the difference + 20 to your AP total. You gun your engines in a sudden upward climb that takes the three Podracers by surprise. You zoom forward over the desert. You may proceed.

If your adventure# is less than 16, subtract the difference from your AP total. You gun your engines in a sudden upward climb, but you're not fast enough. The three Podracers all climb with you. To dive, roll the 10-dice. Your new roll# + your navigation# + your vehicle's stealth# is your new adventure#.

If your new adventure# is equal to or more than 8, add the difference to your AP total. You dive under the other Podracers just in time. You may proceed.

If your new adventure# is less than 8, you couldn't dive out of the way fast enough. To try to get out of the way again, roll the 10-dice again.

> *If your new roll# is equal to or more than 4,* you must try to thread your way through the Podracers (above).

> *If your new roll# is less than 4,* the other Podracers close in on your vehicle, denting it. Subtract 1 from your vehicle's stealth# for the rest of this adventure. Go back to "To dive roll the 10-dice" and repeat until you're past the three Podracers.

Faster.

Directly ahead of you is the green Podracer of the treacherous Gasgano. You veer right to pass.

Gasgano promptly veers right, too, directly in front of you.

Left.

Blocked again.

Right.

Nope.

Gasgano is much quicker than the three Podracers you just passed. You see that the canyon dune turn is approaching— a sharp cliff that will subtly change the air current flow. If you wait, you may have more maneuvering room. But if you get by him now, you'll be that much farther ahead.

Choose to either outflank Gasgano, force him to move off course, or wait until Gasgano passes over the cliff.

To try to outflank Gasgano: Roll the 20-dice. Your roll# + your navigation# + your vehicle's stealth# is your adventure#.

If your adventure# is equal to or more than 15, add the difference + 21 to your AP total. You make a sharp fake to the right, then suddenly thrust left. Gasgano is taken totally by surprise. You may proceed.

If your adventure# is less than 15, subtract the difference from your AP total. You try to pass him on the left, using brute force. But

Gasgano is the bigger brute, and he cuts you off. To try and fake Gasgano again, roll the 10-dice. Your new roll# + your navigation# + your stealth# is your new adventure#.

If your new adventure# is equal to or more than 8, add the difference to your AP total. You make a sharp fake to the right, fake again to the left, then dart to the right. Gasgano's head spins. You may proceed.

If your new adventure# is less than 8, subtract the difference from your AP total. You slip by Gasgano, but he bangs into your starboard engine, forcing you to back off. Choose to either force him off course (below) or wait until he passes over the cliff (below).

To try to force Gasgano off course: Roll the 20-dice. Your roll# + your navigation# + your vehicle's stealth# + your vehicle's speed# is your adventure#.

If your adventure# is equal to or more than 16, add the difference + 21 to your AP total. You sneak up to the port side of Gasgano's Podracer and bank to the right. He tries to steer away and pull ahead, but you match his speed. Soon, he has to veer to avoid a massive sand dune—and goes off course. You may proceed.

If your adventure# is less than 16, subtract 15 from your AP total. You sneak up to the port side of Gasgano's Podracer and bank to the right. But you're not forceful or quick enough and he steers out of the way. You have to veer away to avoid crashing—and Gasgano races ahead. To try and get ahead again, roll the 10-dice.

> *If you roll 1, 2, 3, or 4,* you must try to outflank Gasgano (above).

> *If you roll 5, 6, 7, or 8,* go back "To try to force Gagano off course," and keep trying until you pass Gasgano. However, each time you fail, you must lose twice the amount of AP you lost previously (i.e., 30 the second time, 60 the third time). If you fail a total of three times, you must subtract 100 points additional from your AP total and start the adventure again from the beginning, using a different character.

> *If you roll 9 or 0,* you sneak up to the port side of Gasgano's Podracer, taking him by surprise. You force

him off course, disqualifying him. Congratulations. If you subtracted 1 from your vehicle's stealth# before, you can add it back now—obviously, your Podracer wasn't damaged that badly. You may proceed.

To wait until Gasgano passes over the cliff: Roll the 20-dice. Your roll# + your navigation# + your vehicle's speed# is your adventure#.

If your adventure# is equal to or more than 15, add the difference + 25 to your AP total. As Gasgano flies over the cliff, his Podracer dips. For a nanosecond, Gasgano's gyroscopic oscillator will need to reset. You gun the accelerator and shoot over the top of Gasgano's Podracer with a burst of engine fire. You may proceed.

If your adventure# is less than 15, subtract the difference from your AP total. As Gasgano flies over the cliff, his Podracer dips. But you don't pull open the throttle fast enough, and you dip, too. Now you must either try to outflank Gasgano or try to force him off course (above).

Crrack! Crrrack!

Your Podracer jerks. Sniper fire!

You glance up toward the sound. Your attackers are lying on a desert cliff, their brown masks and tunics camouflaging all but the rifle barrels that glint in the harsh sunlight.

Tusken Raiders. The Sand People. Tatooine natives, bent on disrupting the race.

You must avoid the Raiders' rifle fire. Choose to either speed out of the Raiders' range or avoid the Raiders' by using evasive maneuvers.

To speed out of the Raiders' range: Roll the 20-dice. If evasion is one of your talents, your roll# + your navigation# + your skill# + your vehicle's speed# + 1 is your adventure#. If evasion is not one of your talents, your roll# + your navigation# + your skill# + your vehicle's speed# is your adventure#.

If your adventure# is equal to or more than 17, add the difference + 16 to your AP total. You activate the emergency boosters, and your Podracer slams forward so fast that you get a seat belt burn. You may proceed.

If your adventure# is less than 17, subtract 20 from your AP total. You've been hit. A bullet has bitten a chunk out of your port engine. Subtract 50 from your AP total and 1 from your vehicle's speed# for the rest of this adventure and proceed to "You soar ahead over the desert"(page 81)—unless you stop to try to repair your engine, with or without using Power

To avoid the Raiders by using evasive maneuvers: Roll the 20-dice. Your roll# + your navigation# + your vehicle's stealth# is your adventure#.

If your adventure# is equal to or more than 15, add the difference + 16 to your AP total. You bank, yaw, climb, and drop. Bullets whiz past you. A Podracer behind you is hit and crashes to the desert. But soon the Tusken Raiders have turned their rifles to closer prey. You made it! Straighten out and proceed to "You soar ahead over the desert" (page 81).

If your adventure# is less than 15, subtract the difference from your AP total. In your haste, you pull the throttle instead of the climbing mechanism. Your Podracer coughs, sputters, and slows down. *Smmmmack!* A Tusken musket shot rips a small hole in your port engine. Subtract 50 from your AP total and 1 from your vehicle's speed# for the rest of this adventure. You may proceed to "You soar ahead over the desert"(page 81)—unless you stop to try to repair your engine, with or without using Power (below).

To try to repair your engine (using Power)*: Choose your Alteration or Repair Power. Roll the 20-dice. If repair is also one of your talents, your roll# + your knowledge# + your skill# + your Power# + your Power's low-resist# + 1 is your adventure#. If repair is not one of your talents, your roll# + your knowledge# + your skill# + your Power# + your Power's low-resist# is your adventure#.

If your adventure# is equal to or more than 16, add the difference + 13 to your AP total. You stay airborne until you see a Podracer pit stop, where you make a quick landing. With the help of the pit droids, you replace the damaged panel with new sheathing. It's not the right color, but who cares? Add 1 back to your vehicle's speed# and you may proceed.

If your adventure# is less than 16, subtract the difference from your AP total. As you land at a Podracer pit stop, you remember you have a spot-welding tool and some scrap behind your seat. You get to work repairing the hole, pushing aside the pit droids who swarm around you—and one of them stumbles in front of the turbine and is sucked in! The engine comes to a screaming halt, and you are in deep poodoo. To work on fixing your Podracer, roll the 10-dice. If repair is one of your talents, your new roll# + your knowledge# + your skill# + your Power# + your Power's low-resist# + 1 is your new adventure#. If repair is not one of your talents, your new roll# + your knowledge# + your skill# + your Power# + your Power's low-resist# is your new adventure#.

If your new adventure# is equal to or more than 11, add the difference + 10 to your AP total. You instruct the remaining droids to remove the droid pieces and repair the turbine, while you work on the sheathing. You quickly fix the Pod and race away. You may proceed.

If your new adventure# is less than 11, subtract 20 from your AP total. You pound your fists into the side of your Podracer, then stomp away, wishing you'd never gotten involved in the first place. Go back "To work on fixing your Podracer," and repeat.

*NOTE: This counts as one of three Power uses you are allowed on this adventure.

To repair your engine (without using Power): Roll the 10-dice. Your roll# + your knowledge# + your skill# is your adventure#.

If your adventure# is equal to or more than 9, add the difference + 13 to your AP total. You stay airborne until you see a Podracer pit stop, where you make a quick landing. With the help of the pit droids, you replace the damaged panel with new sheathing. It's not the right color, but who cares? Add 1 to your vehicle's speed# and you may proceed.

If your adventure# is less than 9, subtract the difference from your AP total. You land immediately and jump out of the Pod. There's a hole in the engine sheathing panel. You need a patch—easily obtainable at a Podracer pit stop, but not here in the desert! To fix your engine, roll the 10-dice again.

If you roll 1, 2, 3, or 4, go back "To repair your engine" and repeat until you have fixed the engine. But do not add 1 to your vehicle's speed# when you're done.

If you roll 5, 6, 7, or 8, you remember you have a spot-welding tool and some usable scraps behind your seat. You quickly weld a piece of scrap onto the hole. You've fixed it! Add 1 to your vehicle's speed# and proceed.

If you roll 9 or 0, you're stuck now! You must fly to the nearest pit stop and use Power (above). If you have already used Power three times on this adventure, you can either subtract 200 from your AP total for an additional Power use, or you can subtract 50 from your AP total and restart this adventure from the beginning.

You soar ahead over the desert. The other racers, rattled by the Tusken Raiders, have been slowed. You close ground fast. They're traveling close together, a clutch of vehicles all jockeying for position.

You grit your teeth. Your engine gauges are all maxed out now.

You reach the others just as they vault over a sand jump—only to be greeted by two massive rock outcroppings.

Quick. Steer to avoid them, either with or without using Power.

To avoid the rocks (using Power)*: Choose your Reflex or Navigation Power. Roll the 20-dice If your engine was not harmed or if it was harmed and repaired in the previous confrontation, your roll# + your navigation# + your vehicle's stealth# + your Power# + your Power's mid-resist# is your adventure#. If you did not bother to fix your engine, your roll# + your navigation# + your Power# + your Power's mid-resist# is your adventure#.

If your adventure# is equal to or more than 14, add the difference + 20 to your AP total. Your reflexes take over. You bank hard and hit the port booster. Your Podracer lurches away safely. You may proceed.

If your adventure# is less than 14, subtract the difference from your AP total. You bank hard—but not hard enough. Your engine clanks against the rock and you're forced to stop. Fortunately you're able to bang the dent out with a hammer, and you climb back on. You're now a little exhausted. Subtract 1 from your navigation# for the rest of this adventure. You may proceed.

*NOTE: This counts as one of three Power uses you are allowed on this adventure.

To avoid the rocks (without using Power): Roll the 10-dice. If your engine was not harmed or if it was harmed and repaired in the previous confrontation, your roll# + your navigation# + your vehicle's stealth# + 2 is your adventure#. If you did not bother to fix your engine, your roll# + your navigation# + your vehicle's stealth# is your adventure#.

If your adventure# is equal to or more than 10, add the difference + 25 to your AP total. Even you can't believe your reflexes. You bank hard and hit the port booster at the same time. Your Podracer lurches away, and you may proceed.

If your adventure# is less than 10, subtract the difference from your AP total. You bank hard—but the wrong way. You vault over the rock and off course. To try to recover, roll the 10-dice.

> *If you roll 1, 2, 3, 4, 5, or 6,* you pull your Podracer back, just before it reaches the disqualification zone. With a burst of speed, you set after the others.

> *If you roll 7, 8, 9, or 0,* you cut the Podracer hard to get back on track, but one of your turbines smashes against the rock, and you crash-land! You have been seriously injured. If you have been seriously injured already on this adventure, you must subtract 200 from your AP total and start the adventure from the beginning, using a different character. If you have not been injured already, subtract 1 from your strength# and try not to get injured again—you're lucky that your Podracer is still intact.

As you accelerate, you see Ody Mandrell in a repair pit. His Podracer is belching smoke.

One down.

You rocket over open dune sea now. Another wreck passes below—Mawhonic's Podracer. The side of his engine is sliced from stem to stern.

Two down.

You struggle to break out of the pack but it's too congested. Any sudden move will be stupid. You lean into the final turn together with the others.

The arena seems to rise up out of the sands. As you speed through, the crowd's lusty roar fires your spirit.

Fode/Beed is shouting your name and rank:

Sixth place.

You have completed one lap of the Boonta Eve Podrace. Add 100 to your AP total.

As you *whoosh* into the second lap, you pull farther ahead in the pack.

Fifth...

You can see Sebulba now. Trading first place with three other racers. They're slowing one another down.

You close ground fast. Directly ahead of you, Mars Guo is closing in on Sebulba.

You make your move to pass Mars.

Sebulba breaks a metal ornament off his Pod and tosses it over his shoulder—directly into Mars's engine.

SCREEEEEEE...

Mars is veering toward you, out of control!

He's spinning violently every which way. Quick, steer away from him!

To avoid Mars Guo: Roll the 10-dice. If reflex is one of your talents, your roll# + your navigation# + your vehicle's stealth# + your knowledge# is your adventure#. If reflex is not one of your talents, your roll# + your navigation# + your vehicle's stealth# is your adventure#.

If your adventure# is equal to or more than 9, add the difference + 19 to your AP total. In your mind, you see where Mars will be going—left—and you choose right. Right is correct! You're in the clear. Now it's you and three other racers, including Sebulba. You may proceed.

If your adventure# is less than 9, subtract 10 from your AP total. You try to steer away, but Mars clips your side. Your Pod spins out of control as a connecting strap snaps loose like a whip. To reach out and try to grab the flying strap on its return, roll the 10-dice again. If reflex is one of your talents, your new roll# + your skill# + your strength# + 1 is your new adventure#. If reflex is not one of your talents, your new roll# + your skill# + your strength# is your new adventure#.

If your new adventure# is equal to or more than 9, add the difference + 5 to your AP total. The strap burns your palm as it strikes—but you grab hard. Swinging it around to your starboard stern, you attach it firmly to the engine. You may proceed.

If your new adventure# is less than 9, subtract the difference from your AP total. The strap slips through your outstretched fingers and flails in the air as your Pod dips wildly. Go back "To reach out and try to grab the flying strap on its return," until you grab the strap.

You've lost time, but your Pod closes ground on the straightaway.

By the end of the second lap, you're on Sebulba's tail. You enter the arena and tear past the stands, barely hearing the roar of the crowd.

You're now on the last lap.

Gauges flash red all over your dashboard. Your engines are overheating. You can't slow down now.

This is going to be the toughest moment of your life. Win, and your new friends will be saved. Lose, and your dreams of glory go up in smoke. Choose to pass Sebulba, either with or without using Power.

To pass Sebulba (using Power)*: Choose your Reflex or Navigation Power. Roll the 20-dice. If navigation is one of your talents and you have chosen Navigation Power, your roll# + your navigation# + your vehicle's stealth# + your vehicle's speed# + your Power# + your Power's mid-resist# + 1 is your adventure#. If navigation is not one of your talents or if you chose Reflex Power, your roll# + your navigation# + your vehicle's stealth# + your vehicle's speed# + your Power# + your Power's mid-resist# is your adventure#.

If your adventure# is equal to or more than 18, add the difference + 25 to your AP total. You rev your Podracer. In a burst of energy, you dart around Sebulba's left side. He picks up speed. You're neck and neck. Proceed to "The Dug is setting the pace," (page 97).

If your adventure# is less than 18, subtract 15 from your AP total. You give your Podracer a burst of energy—but it's not enough. You go to pass Sebulba, but he blocks your move. You're stuck. To figure out another strategy, roll the 10-dice. Your new roll# + your navigation# + your knowledge# + your vehicle's speed# is your new adventure#.

If your new adventure# is equal to or more than 9, add the difference + 10 to your AP total. You draw Sebulba to the right with a sharp thrust—and then you move to his left, quickly pulling beside him. You're neck and neck! Proceed to "The Dug is setting the pace," (page 97).

If your new adventure# is less than 9, subtract 10 from your AP total. You freeze. You can't decide what to do. You will need to look at the number you just rolled.

If you roll 1, 2, or 3, you must go "To pass Sebulba without using Power," (below).

If you roll 4, proceed "To outflank Sebulba," (page 92).

If you roll 5, you try to swing to the side —but there's a rock right there! Your Podracer hits and you are thrown from the cockpit, seriously injured. If you have been seriously injured already on this adventure, you must subtract 200 from your AP total and start the adventure from the beginning, using another character. If you have not been injured already, subtract 1 from your strength# and try not to get injured again. You climb back into your Podracer and are glad to see it starts like a charm. You manage to get within range of Sebulba again. Go "To pass Sebulba (using Power)," (below).

If you roll 6, 7, or 8, proceed "To pass above Sebulba," (page 94).

If you roll 9 or 0, proceed "To pass beneath Sebulba," (page 96).

*NOTE: This counts as one of three Power uses you are allowed on this adventure.

To pass Sebulba (without using Power): Roll the 20-dice. If navigation is one of your talents, your roll# + your navigation# + your vehicle's stealth# + your vehicle's speed# + 1 is your adventure#. If navigation is not one of your talents, your roll# + your navigation# + your vehicle's stealth# + your vehicle's speed# is your adventure#.

If your adventure# is equal to or more than 15, add the difference + 25 to your AP total. You fake trying to go over him, then under him. He lifts and drops to block you. Then, at the precise moment he's dropping, you shoot around his left side. You're now neck and neck! Proceed to "The Dug is setting the pace," (page 97).

If your adventure# is less than 15, subtract the difference from your AP total. You're quick, but Sebulba is quicker. He blocks your every move. To try again, roll the 10-dice. Your new roll# + your navigation# + your vehicle's stealth# + your vehicle's speed# + 1 is your new adventure#.

If your new adventure# is equal to or more than 10, add the difference + 15 to your AP total. You draw Sebulba to the right with a sharp thrust—and then you move to his left, quickly pulling beside him. You're now neck and neck! Proceed to "The Dug is setting the pace," (page 97).

If your new adventure# is less than 10, subtract 15 from your AP total. You freeze. You can't decide what to do. Look at the number you just rolled.

If you roll 1, 2, or 3, proceed "To out-flank Sebulba," (below).

If you roll 4, you must try to pass Sebulba using Power (above). If you have already used Power three times on this adventure, you can either subtract 200 from your AP total for an additional Power use, or you can subtract 50 from your AP total and restart this adventure from the beginning.

If you roll 5, 6, 7, or 8, proceed "To pass above Sebulba," (page 94).

If you roll 9 or 0, Proceed "To pass beneath Sebulba" (page 96).

To outflank Sebulba: Roll the 20-dice. Your roll# + your navigation# + your stealth# + your vehicle's stealth# is your adventure#.

If your adventure# is equal to or more than 16, add the difference + 25 to your AP total. You fake repeatedly, with a steady rhythm.

Sebulba follows every swing—and then you catch him by surprise. Faking right, you zoom around to his left. You're neck and neck! You may proceed.

If your adventure# is less than 16, subtract 15 from your AP total. No matter what you try, Sebulba blocks you. Roll the 10-dice.

> *If you roll 1, 2, 3, or 4,* subtract 1 from your skill# for the rest of this adventure and proceed "To pass above Sebulba," (below).

> *If you roll 5, 6, or 7,* you fake right and then go left, pulling beside Sebulba. You're neck and neck! You may proceed.

> *If you roll 8,* you try to swing to the side—but there's a rock right there! Your Podracer hits and you are thrown from the cockpit, seriously injured. If you have been seriously injured already on this adventure, you must subtract 200 from your AP total and start the adventure from the beginning, using a different character. If you have not been injured already, subtract 1 from your strength# for the rest of this adventure

and try not to get injured again. You climb back into your Podracer and are glad to see that it starts like a charm. You manage to get within range of Sebulba again. Go back "To pass Sebulba (without using Power)", (above).

If you roll 9 or 0, you fake right and then go left around Sebulba—but you're too close. He rams into you and you lurch to the side. Subtract 1 from your vehicle's distance# for the rest of this adventure and you may proceed.

To pass above Sebulba: Roll the 10-dice. If navigation is one of your talents, your roll# + your navigation# + your vehicle's speed# + 1 is your adventure#. If navigation is not one of your talents, your roll# + your navigation# + your vehicle's speed# is your adventure#.

If your adventure# is equal to or more than 9, add the difference + 30 to your AP total. Sebulba doesn't expect the move. You zoom overhead, and he zooms up beside you. You're neck and neck! You may proceed.

If your adventure# is less than 9, subtract 30 from your AP total. Sebulba anticipates your move. If you've already tried going from side to side, you must try to pass Sebulba by going underneath him (below). If you haven't already tried going from side to side, roll the 10-dice.

If you roll 1, 2, 3, or 4, try to outflank Sebulba (above).

If you roll 5, 6, or 7, try to pass beneath Sebulba (below).

If you roll 8, you try to swing to the side—but there's a rock right there! Your Podracer hits and you are thrown from the cockpit, seriously injured. If you have been seriously injured already on this adventure, you must subtract 200 from your AP total and start the adventure from the beginning, using a different character. If you have not been injured already, subtract 1 from your strength# for the rest of this adventure and try not to get injured again. You climb back into your Podracer and are glad to see that it starts like a charm. You manage to get within range of Sebulba again. Go back "To pass Sebulba (without using Power)," (above).

If you roll 9 or 0, one more time: Fake low, go high. This time, you pass overhead! But you're too close. Sebulba rams into you. Your Podracer wobbles, and you drop to his side. Subtract 1 from your vehicle's distance# for the rest of this adventure and you may proceed.

To pass beneath Sebulba: Roll the 10-dice. If reflex is one of your talents, your roll# + your navigation# + your stealth# + your vehicle's stealth# is your adventure#. If reflex is not one of your talents, your roll# + your navigation# + your vehicle's stealth# is your adventure#.

If your adventure# is equal to or more than 10, add the difference + 25 to your AP total. Sebulba doesn't expect the move. You zoom under him, and for a moment he can't see you. Then you come up beside him—and you're neck and neck! You may proceed.

If your adventure# is less than 10, subtract 15 from your AP total. Sebulba anticipates your move and blocks you again. Roll the 10-dice again. If navigation is one of your talents, your new roll# + your navigation# + your stealth# + your vehicle's speed# + 1 is your new adventure#. If navigation is not one of your talents, your new roll# + your navigation# + your vehicle's speed# + 1 is your new adventure#.

If your new adventure# is equal to or more than 10, add the difference + 25 to your AP total. You fake repeatedly, with a steady rhythm. Sebulba follows every swing— and then you catch him by surprise. Faking right, you zoom around to his left. You're neck and neck! You may proceed.

If your new adventure# is less than 10, subtract 10 from your AP total. You fake right and then go left around Sebulba— but you're too close. He rams into you and you lurch to the side, jolted considerably. Subtract 1 from your navigation# for the rest of this adventure and you may proceed.

The Dug is setting the pace, not letting you get ahead. Suddenly you see a flame burst from Sebulba's vent ports. It shears through the side of your engine.

You yank the controls to the left.

The Podracer banks. You're on the edge of the course, headed right toward the service ramp!

With a controlled thrust, you lurch back on course—and ahead of Sebulba!

The desert stretches out before you, wide and empty. You pull back the throttle, but it's already at full. No turbine can withstand such sustained strain.

Thunk.

The Podracer jumps. You glance behind you and see Sebulba on your tail, trying to bump you off course.

Thunk.

Your engine gauge begins to flash. One of the resistors has gone. You'll need auxiliary power.

That's when you remember. That nagging feeling—the thing you knew you hadn't done—was to fix the auxiliary-power shifter! If you don't let it out at exactly the right speed, it will stall.

You have no choice now. You must switch to auxiliary mode.

To switch the damaged engine to auxiliary power: Roll the 20-dice. Your roll# + your knowledge# + your skill# + 1 is your adventure#.

If your adventure# is equal to or more than 15, add the difference + 33 to your AP total. You put your hand on the shifter and try to recall how it felt to pull it correctly. You take it easy, letting your instincts be your guide— and VOOM! The starboard engine cuts off and you shift into auxiliary mode with a burst of speed! You may proceed.

If your adventure# is less than 15, subtract the difference from your AP total. You yank the shifter back—and your starboard engine coughs and goes dead. You're listing to port. To quickly try again, roll the 10-dice. Your new roll# + your knowledge# + your skill# is your new adventure#.

>*If your new adventure# is equal to or more than 8,* add the difference to your AP total. You put your hand on the shifter and try to recall how it felt to pull it correctly. You take it easy, letting your instincts be your guide—and VOOM! The main engine cuts off and you shift into auxiliary mode with a burst of speed! You may proceed.

>*If your new adventure# is less than 8,* subtract 15 from your AP total. You try to slow it down, but you're too jumpy. Your Podracer is spiraling into a nosedive. Go back "To quickly try again," and repeat

until you manage to activate the auxiliary power.

Sebulba has pulled into the lead. But with a fresh power source, you're soon on his tail again.

The end of the race is near. Sebulba is no match for your reflexes, and you pass around his starboard side.

You're engine to engine now. You slowly pull ahead.

Sebulba nudges right.

Smack!

Your Podracer jolts.

Smack!

Sebulba is bouncing against you now, a little harder each time. You struggle to keep on course.

Smack!

Smack!

CLICK!

Suddenly, the bouncing stops. The two Podracers' steering arms are locked together.

Ahead of you is the arena, just coming over the horizon line.

Sebulba grins.

If you stay like this, it's a sure tie.

This is the worst thing Sebulba can do. Worse than knocking you off course.

It's a coward's choice.

If Sebulba wants this race, he will have to earn it. Choose to either pry apart the steering arms either by using a crowbar, by pulling away from Sebulba, by changing your speed until they unhook, or by using Power.

To pry apart the steering arms with a crowbar: Roll the 20-dice. Your roll# + your strength# + your skill# + 1 is your adventure#.

If your adventure# is equal to or more than 17, add the difference + 30 to your AP total. You pull the crowbar from under your seat, reach over the side of the cockpit, and jam it between the rods. *Crrrrunch!* The two Podracers lunge away from each other. Your steering arm hangs in shreds by the port side. You're separated, but now neither of you can steer! You may proceed.

If your adventure# is less than 17, subtract the difference from your AP total. You pull the crowbar out from under your seat, reach over the side of the Pod, and jam it between the rods. But they're jammed too tight. Roll the 10-dice.

> *If you roll 1, 2, or 3,* proceed to separate the steering arms by pulling your Podracer away from Sebulba (below).

> *If you roll 4,* as you're trying to pry apart the steering arms, you lean over too far and lose control of the Podracer! It veers off course and you are thrown from the cockpit, seriously injured. If you have been seriously injured already on this adventure, you must subtract 200 from your AP total and start the adventure from the beginning, using a different character. If you have not been injured already, subtract 1 from your strength# for the rest of this adventure and try not to get injured again. You manage to cling to the Podracer as it races on. Proceed "To pull your Podracer away from Sebulba," (below).

> *If you roll 5, 6, 7, or 8,* proceed "To vary speed until the steering arms unhook," (below).

If you roll 9 or 0, choose to either go back to "Roll the 10-dice" and keep trying until you get loose (above), or use Power (page 106).

To pull your Podracer away from Sebulba: Roll the 20-dice and grapple with the controls. Your roll# + your strength# + your skill# + your vehicle's stealth# is your adventure#.

If your adventure# is equal to or more than 17, add the difference + 30 to your AP total. You cut the steering wheel hard to starboard. The rods bend, groaning with the strain. You cut again, sharper…*crrrrunch!* The two Podracers lunge away from each other. Your steering arm hangs in shreds by the port side. You're separated, but now neither of you can steer! You may proceed.

If your adventure# is less than 17, subtract the difference from your AP total. You cut the steering wheel hard to starboard. The rods bend, groaning with the strain. You cut again, sharper—but Sebulba's pulling, too, and harder. Quickly, try to vary speeds until the steering arms unhook (below).

To vary speeds until the steering arms unhook: Roll the 10-dice. Your roll# + your navigation# + your skill# + 1 is your adventure#.

If your adventure# is equal to or more than 9, add the difference + 30 to your AP total. You move the throttle back and forth. The two Podracers jerk sharply. The rods groan with the strain, gradually slipping away from each other, until...*crrrrunch!* The rods break. The Podracers lunge away from each other. Your steering arm hangs in shreds by the port side. You're separated, but now neither of you can steer! You may proceed.

If your adventure# is less than 9, subtract the difference from your AP total. You move the throttle back and forth. The two Podracers jerk sharply. But the rods are stubborn—and strong. You and Sebulba are fast approaching the arena. Roll the 10-dice again. Your new roll# + your navigation# + your skill# + your strength# + your vehicle's speed# is your new adventure#.

If your new adventure# is equal to or more than 12, add the difference to your AP total. Sebulba can't do this. He can't steal a win from you. Furious, you yank and push the throttle as hard as you can until...

crrrunch! The rods break. The Podracers lunge away from each other. Your steering arm hangs in shreds by the port side. You're separated, but now neither of you can steer! You may proceed.

If your new adventure# is less than 12, subtract 15 from your AP total. This isn't working. You are about to tie. Look at the number you just rolled.

> *If you roll 1, 2, or 3,* you have no choice but to pull the steering arms apart using Power (below). If you have already used Power three times on this adventure, choose to either subtract 400 from your AP total for another Power use, or you can subtract 200 from your AP total and restart this adventure from the beginning.

> *If you roll 4 or 5,* go "To pull your Podracer away from Sebulba," back (page 103).

> *If you roll 6 or 7,* Sebulba turns to you with a slimy grin and mouths the word "Peedunkel." *Slave child.* You boil inside—but of course he's right. You are a slave boy. This race is the only glory you'll ever have. Your eye is on the finish line and you pull the throttle back to

max. With a sudden *crrrrunch*, the rods break. The Podracers lunge away from each other. Your steering arm hangs in shreds by the port side. You're separated, but now neither of you can steer! You may proceed.

If you roll 9 or 0, you're heading for one of the arena watchtowers! You can't think of Sebulba now, only about your own life. You steer sharply away, but Sebulba's pushing back hard. Suddenly, as you're about to hit, you hear a *crrrrunch*. The rods break and the Podracers lunge away from each other. You miss the tower, but your steering arm hangs in shreds by the port side, and you can't steer! You may proceed.

To pull the steering arms apart (using Power)*: Choose your Acceleration or Alteration Power. Roll the 20-dice. Your roll# + your navigation# + your skill# + your vehicle's speed# + your Power# + your Power's mid-resist# is your adventure#.

If your adventure# is equal to or more than 19, add the difference + 30 to your AP total. You accelerate so suddenly that the rods can't take the strain. With a loud *crrrrunch*, they break. The Podracers lunge away from each other. Your steering arm hangs in shreds by the port side. You're separated, but now neither of you can steer! You may proceed.

If your adventure# is less than 19, subtract 15 from your AP total. You accelerate sharply—but not quickly enough to break the steering arms. Instead, you're pulling Sebulba along with you! He turns to you with a slimy grin and mouths the word "Peedunkel"—slave child—and you lose your temper. Roll the 10-dice.

> *If you roll 1, 2, 3, 4, or 5,* this time you accelerate so suddenly that the rods can't take the strain. With a loud *crrrrunch*, they break. The Podracers lunge away from each other. Your steering arm hangs in shreds by the port side. You're separated, but now neither of you can steer! You may proceed.

> *If you roll 6,* as you're trying to pry apart the steering arms, you lean over too far and lose control of the Podracer! It veers off course and you are thrown from the cockpit, seriously injured. If you have been seriously injured already on this adventure, you must subtract 200 from your AP total and start the

adventure from the beginning, using a different character. If you have not been injured already, subtract 1 from your strength# for the rest of this adventure and try not to get injured again. You manage to cling to the Podracer as it races on. Try to separate the steering arms by pulling your Podracer away from Sebulba (page 103).

If you roll 7, 8, 9, or 0, Sebulba takes advantage of your lapse of concentration to make a sudden move of his own to pull away. With a loud *crrrrunch*, the rods break. The Podracers lunge away from each other. Your steering arm hangs in shreds by the port side. You're separated, but now neither of you can steer! You may proceed.

*NOTE: This counts as one of three Power uses you are allowed on this adventure.

You scream. The desert and sky are a spinning blur around you. The Podracer is uncontrollable, racing forward blindly.

On the recoil, Sebulba arcs high and fast toward a towering rock outcropping near the outskirts of the Mos Espa arena. He quickly rights the Pod.

His port engine, however, is not so lucky.

It smashes against the rock, caroming back to hit the starboard engine. With a boom that echoes through the plain, both turbines explode into flames. Sebulba's Pod thrusts forward on its own momentum, without the engines, coming to a rest just inside the arena.

Then, there is a second explosion. Softer but growing louder by the nanosecond. An explosion of voices and cheers and beeps and whistles and musical instruments.

"THE PEEDUNKEL WINS!" bellows Fode/Beed.

You hurtle into the arena. Alone.

"YOU DID IT! YOU DID IT! YOU DID IT!"

Your best friend's shouting drowns out all other sounds. But you don't mind. Not a bit. You feel yourself being lifted high in the air. You see a blur of faces—an, brown, blue, green, mottled, smooth—creatures from all over the Outer Rim, smiling with admiration and recognition. They know you now. They know who you are. From now on, you will no longer be the Peedunkel, the slave child.

Instead, you will forever be the youngest victor in history of the Boonta Eve Classic.

Congratulations! You have completed all your goals, by winning the Podrace. Add 500 to your AP total.

To read the end of this adventure, turn to page 60 of your *Star Wars* Adventures novel, *Podrace to Freedom*.